Summer at Sea

Summer at Sea

CLIFFORD Q. EDWARDS

WORD BOOKS,
Publisher
Waco, Texas

SUMMER AT SEA

Printed in the United States of America
ISBN 0-87680-836-4
Library of Congress catalog card number: 73-84576

First Paperback Printing, September 1976

To my Jim and everybody's Fraser

Contents

1.
Getting Started

"Good-by, mama, good-by, papa, good-by, Kathy," called Manuel as the train glided out of the station, slowly at first, then rapidly gaining speed. In just a moment it rounded a curve, and nothing was left but a tiny plume of smoke which hung in the heavy salt air. Manuel turned quickly to his grandfather, "Now we can go, gramp. We'd better hurry before the grocery store closes."

"I think we'll make it in time, son," said Cap'n Tony dryly. "It's only four-thirty, and the stores don't close till six. Besides, we're only a few blocks away, and we have a car right here to take us." And Cap'n Tony smiled at his young grandson, skipping beside him. "I know you're excited about going on the *Miss Abbie* for the summer, but just take it easy. Everything will come out all right."

"You know, gramp," said Manuel, suddenly shy, "I've always wanted to go shrimping with you on the *Miss Abbie,* but you always said I was too little. When you took all of us to ride on the *Miss Abbie* last month for the blessing of the fleet that Sunday, I felt like I couldn't stand it if I didn't get to be with you this summer. Then when papa had to go away on a business trip this whole vacation, I was so afraid that I was still too little for you to take me. It's hard to believe that in one short year I've suddenly grown big enough for you to trust me on board your boat for three months."

"You haven't done all this growing in one short year, boy," said gramp. "It's been happening all the time, and you just didn't realize it. I always figured when you were tall enough not to get your teeth caught in my belt buckle you'd be old enough to go to sea with me!"

Involuntarily, Manuel glanced down at his grandfather's belt buckle, then caught the man's eyes on him as he looked up, and both burst out laughing.

"If I'd known that was your measuring stick, I'd have tried to get you to wear suspenders!" cried Manuel as they reached gramp's car and climbed inside.

Gramp started the motor, and off they rattled down the bumpy street that led from the train station to the business section. Brunswick was a sleepy little town

located on the Brunswick River close to the coast of southeast Georgia. Many Portuguese families resided there, and their men usually shrimped for a living. The street ran parallel to the river, and there were boats tied up at the docks in the late afternoon sun. Overhead seagulls wheeled about, squawking greetings to each other as they passed the time of day. The pungent clean smell of tar mingled with the dank odor of salt river mud, but these sights and sounds were so familiar to the two in the old car that they passed unnoticed.

Soon they pulled up in front of the new supermarket. As they started inside, Manuel asked, "What are we going to buy, gramp? I know there is a stove on board the *Miss Abbie,* but do we cook on it like mama does at home?"

"Yes, there is a stove, and we cook on it, but not quite the same food or the same way," replied gramp. "There is no oven—only burners on the top, so we can't get anything that needs baking or roasting. We can boil, stew, and fry things so good that your mouth will water just smelling 'em. What do you like best in that line, Manuel? I like 'most anything, so suppose we let you do the selecting this first time."

This was such a new experience to Manuel that he stood blank. His mother had a list and always bought from that. What did you get for meals?

"While you're thinking," said gramp, "suppose we start with bread, butter, eggs, and milk. Then you'll see things that you'll want as we go along."

Gramp was right. As they wandered around the lanes, their buggy became more and more heaped. By the time they reached the check-out station, Manuel had a hard time seeing over the top.

"Golly!" breathed Manuel, "that ought to last us all summer and still have some left over."

"You'd be surprised," laughed Cap'n Tony. "When you live on a shrimp boat and do a man's work and eat three meals a day, the pantry gets empty faster than you'd think. Well, come on, let's take our groceries and get on down to the *Miss Abbie*. By the time we get things put away and I show you over the boat, it'll be time to eat supper, wash the dishes, and go to sleep. You know, we have to get up around two o'clock in the morning. Believe me, that time of day surely does come early!"

It took just a short while to drive to the dock where the *Miss Abbie* was tied. As they stepped aboard, Manuel admired her gleaming white sides, the tidy coils of line on the deck, and shiny brass of her fittings. They went first to the galley where Cap'n Tony showed Manuel how to stack the groceries in the tiny pantry and the refrigerator. Then Cap'n Tony turned to the little gas stove.

"What's the railing around the stove for?" asked Manuel.

"To keep the pots from sliding off when you're cooking in a heavy sea," replied Cap'n Tony. "Look at this cabinet here where the dishes are. See, all the shelves have railings in front of them. When the sea gets rolling, no dish or pot could set still. You'll notice that everything is bolted to the deck—the table and chairs in here, the bunks in the cabin, everything."

Manuel took stock of each thing as his grandfather pointed it out. He also noticed how compact everything was—room for everything but no wasted space. Next they went to the cabin where there were two double bunks and unpacked their suitcases and put their clothes in the chest.

"Can we go up front next, gramp?" asked Manuel.

"Now, son," said Cap'n Tony kindly, "you're going to be living on board this boat all summer, so you might as well start talking like a seaman instead of a landlubber. On a boat you say forward instead of up front. When you go to the back of the boat, you call it the stern, and you go aft to get there. The kitchen is the galley, and the bathroom is the head, and there are no floors on a boat—they're all decks. When you meet Jerry tomorrow, you'll hear how he speaks. The first thing you know, you'll be talking like an old salt, yourself."

"Jerry is your striker, isn't he, gramp?" asked Manuel.

"Yes he is, son, and one of the best. He came to work for me when he wasn't much bigger than you are. He's saving his money to buy a shrimp boat and learning the trade as he makes the money to set himself up."

As they talked, the two walked forward to the pilot-house where the big, spoked steering wheel was located. This section was enclosed in glass windows which would slide open to let in the fresh sea breeze or close tightly to keep out the salt spray when the wind and waves were high. In front of the big wheel was the compass, set in liquid so it stayed level even when the boat was pitching and tossing at sea. Over the door next to the wheel was a .22 rifle in a rack.

"What's that for, gramp?" Manuel asked.

"In case we need it for anything," answered Cap'n Tony. "If we caught a big whipray in the net, we'd have to shoot it before we could haul the net on board. Those things are heavy and dangerous, too. Of course, we don't often catch 'em, but it's good to have a rifle in case we do. Or in case of sharks—anything. You never know when you'll need a gun on a shrimp boat, and it's a good idea to have it."

Next they went below to the engine room, and Cap'n Tony showed Manuel the big beautiful diesel engine which ran the boat. Then they went back on deck to the stern of the boat, and Manuel looked at the big net hanging from its pulleys high above him.

"Exactly how does that work, gramp?" asked Manuel.

"The net has a long line on it which is connected to this electric hoist," explained gramp. "To let it out into the water, we push a release button which allows the line to go out slowly. This lets the net out farther and farther behind the boat. You'll notice there's a big board on either side of the net. Each board is weighted, so as the net goes out, the weighted end of the board sinks down. These boards are rigged so they spread out in opposite directions from the net—the one on the right goes 'way out to starboard, and the left one goes to port. This keeps the net open wide, and when we drag, the shrimp will be caught. When we think we have dragged long enough, we press this button, here, and the net comes in to the boat and is hoisted aboard.

"In olden times the fishermen and shrimpers had to pull their nets by hand, but somebody invented the electric pulleys and hoist, and now all the modern shrimp boats use them."

"That saves a lot of work, doesn't it?" asked Manuel.

"It not only saves a lot of work, but it lets us use much bigger nets and catch many more shrimp each drag," replied Cap'n Tony. "Without them, we wouldn't catch a tenth as many."

Manuel looked up at the big net, suspended from its hoist against the blue sky, and asked, "What are those red, yellow, and black things?"

"They are mats made from polyethylene rope," answered the captain. "We buy this rope by the pound and weave the line into the net to keep it from dragging on the bottom of the ocean. Shells of all kinds are there, and some have very sharp edges, especially oysters. The mats are under the net and help to protect it from being caught and torn by the shells. Even so, sometimes it is caught on a reef and torn in spite of the mats. That's bad, for then the shrimp find the holes and escape. You can usually tell when this happens for the boat will be jerked and sometimes almost stopped by the pull. Then we bring the net aboard and mend it as quickly as we can. Every afternoon when we get back to the dock we look it over to see if this has happened when we didn't know it, or if any lines have worn loose. If so, we mend it then for the next day."

"I didn't know there was so much to this business," said Manuel. "Where do you keep the shrimp that you catch first so they don't spoil?"

Cap'n Tony pulled aside a hatch in the deck. "This is the hold," he said. "Every afternoon the ice truck comes by and loads it for the next day's shrimping.

We sort through every catch. The shrimp are headed and put in here as well as any fish large enough to keep. We sell these to the quick-freeze people, and our shrimp and fish are shipped frozen all over the country to people who can't buy them fresh."

"Speaking of fish," said Manuel, "is it too early to have supper? I'm hungry."

Cap'n Tony looked at his watch and was surprised to see how late it was. "No, indeed," he replied. "Come on, let's go to the galley and see what we'll eat tonight."

They decided on hot dogs, sauerkraut, and buns, and Cap'n Tony showed Manuel how to light the little gas stove. Supper was soon ready, and never had hot dogs tasted so good before. Manuel ate three, and Cap'n Tony ate four!

The few dirty dishes were soon washed, dried, and put away. Cap'n Tony and Manuel went to the cabin. One of the upper bunks looked good to Manuel, and he undressed and climbed up into it. Cap'n Tony took his usual bottom bunk, turned out the light, and all was quiet.

Manuel lay still and didn't say a word. Soon he could hear his grandfather breathing as though he was asleep, but Manuel was too excited to sleep. The *Miss Abbie* rocked slightly with the motion of the river. There were many strange sounds—captains of other boats tied up alongside, talking in low tones, boats bumping lightly against the dock, the bark of a dog

17

that lived on a boat close by. This was all different from what he was used to. Manuel lay listening to everything and thinking, "Will morning never come?"

2.
Arrival of Footsie

The next thing Manuel knew, Cap'n Tony was shaking him and saying, "Wake up, boy. You can't lie there and sleep all day. We've got work to do. Those shrimp won't wait for us, and if we eat, we have to work."

Manuel hopped down from his bunk to see gramp standing there already dressed. Breakfast was on the little table in the galley, and he could smell the wonderful bacon and eggs. "I'll be ready in a minute," he said as he snatched on his clothes and ran to the head to wash his face.

"Don't worry, Manuel," laughed Cap'n Tony. "I won't leave you! Come eat breakfast as soon as you're ready, and we'll get underway."

When breakfast was over, Cap'n Tony and Manuel stepped across the railing and stood on the dock.

There they were joined by Jerry, gramp's striker. All around them was the bustle of the men of the shrimp fleet, getting ready in the early morning darkness to set out for the day's work.

"Jerry," said Cap'n Tony; "all this time I've done the teaching and you've done the learning. Let's see how well you can teach Manuel to cast off."

By the lights on the dock, Jerry gave Manuel his first lesson. He released the bow line from the piling of the dock, then instructed Manuel to release the stern line as soon as the engine was running steadily. When he called to Manuel to cast off, the boy had a job to work the heavy line up and over the piling. Several times he pinched his fingers, but he didn't say a word. He was afraid Cap'n Tony would think he was soft and be sorry for the summer plans.

When he finally had the line freed from the piling, Manuel was out of breath. He jumped back on board the boat and went into the pilothouse with his grandfather. As soon as the boat was headed out to sea, Jerry showed Manuel how to coil the line on deck in a neat pile. In this way, he said, the line would not get fouled up with anything else on deck. It would be out of the way so nobody would trip over it, and it would be ready to use when they reached the dock that afternoon. Manuel began to realize that this summer would not be all play. There was work to be done and lots of it. He felt proud that his granddad would take him on as a second striker.

When Manuel finished coiling the line on deck, he and Jerry joined gramp and watched him steer the big boat down the broad Brunswick River in the darkness. Cap'n Tony pointed out the buoy lights and explained how he lined up these lights and steered from them so the boat would stay in the deep channel and not run aground. Manuel listened carefully, then asked Cap'n Tony to let him try steering.

"Not yet, son," replied the man. "I will when I think you're ready for it, but this water is tricky and it's a little too soon for you to start steering. If you learn as fast as I think you will, it won't be long before you and Jerry'll be doing all the work and I'll just lie in the cabin and sleep!"

All three laughed at this picture, but Manuel vowed silently that he would listen and learn as fast as he could. Then he would surprise his granddad one day and take the *Miss Abbie* in and out the river all by himself.

The three sat in silence in the darkness of the pilothouse. Manuel was fascinated by the bobbing lights of the buoys and the sure way that gramp handled the big wheel. Gramp's feet were planted firmly in front of it, and he seemed barely to grasp the spokes, but as the boat slid swiftly along, Manuel noticed there was no jerking or swaying—only smooth gliding. He looked out of the pilothouse, and ahead and behind were strings of lights from the other boats in the fleet, all headed out to sea. The river widened and gradually merged into St. Simons Sound as they moved between St. Simons Island on the north and Jekyll Island on the south. Time passed and the sky started to grow light. One by one the stars disappeared, and soon it was light enough to see the birds flying all around. Then Cap'n Tony said, "It won't be long now until we can put the net over for the first drag."

Lowering the net overboard was something else new to Manuel. He watched Jerry carefully, and the net slowly slipped from sight into the Atlantic Ocean. The striker kept paying out the line until it was all gone, then they went back to the pilothouse. There was nothing to do on this first drag but wait until time to hoist the net to the boat. After the first drag there would be plenty of work—picking out the shrimp, heading and throwing them into the iced hold, saving the larger fish, separating the big blue crabs, then cleaning the deck and washing it down for the next haul. But for this drag, all they had to do was ride slowly up and down the ocean where the shrimp were swimming silently and unseen underneath.

Manuel was impatient to see what they caught in this drag, but Cap'n Tony said, "Just hold your seahorses, boy. You won't be so anxious after you see what has to be done when the net is brought on board."

Finally Cap'n Tony decided they had trawled enough, so he put the boat in neutral gear, and Jerry pushed the button that started winding the net in. Manuel's eyes nearly popped out of his head when he saw how many shrimp, fish, and crabs were in the bag. Jerry untied the line at the bottom of the net, and it emptied onto the deck. He looked around just in time to see Manuel jumping and hopping for dear life to get out of the way of a huge blue crab that was scuttling straight for the boy's bare toes. He started laughing, and when Manuel was sure he was safe, he laughed too. Those pinching crab claws were something to be avoided!

Cap'n Tony showed Manuel how to hold the shrimp with one hand and quickly pull the head off with the other. The shrimp were tossed into one pile and the heads on another, then he left the boys to finish the job. He put the boat in gear again, and the net was lowered for another drag.

Manuel worked as hard as he could, but he thought he would never learn to be as quick as Jerry. Every time he looked at the big pile of unheaded shrimp it seemed just as large as before. His back began to ache from bending over so much, and his fingers had dozens of little stinging pricks from being stuck by the horns in the heads and tails of the shrimp. Finally, however, the last shrimp was headed, and all were put into the iced hold. Then Jerry took a bucket with a line on it, dropped the bucket overboard, and pulled it back full of water. This he used to pour on the deck, and all the waste was washed into the sea through the openings at the stern.

Seagulls of all kinds had been following the boat lazily, but when the deck was washed, they suddenly darted down behind the boat. Such screaming and squawking Manuel had never heard! It sounded as though a radio had gone crazy with screeching static as they dipped and dived, fighting each other for their food! While he watched them, Manuel rested and massaged his sore fingers, and soon he felt as good as new.

After the second drag was hauled on board, he worked a little faster. Though his fingers still stung and his back still ached, he felt proud. When it was time for lunch, he made the sandwiches and coffee and took them to his granddad who was steering. Jerry brought out his lunch, and the three ate together.

The day passed all too quickly, and before Manuel knew it, his grandad was saying, "Well, that's the last drag for today. Don't you think we've done enough?"

It was good to see by daylight the way they had come in darkness that morning. Long before they reached the dock the boys had the deck all cleared and clean. When the boat pulled up at her berth, Manuel felt as though he had been at sea all his life, but by bedtime he was too tired to care. Unlike the night before, he pulled himself slowly up into his bunk.

He was just drifting off to sleep when he realized

24

he heard something. There were so many strange noises all around that he had to hear this particular one repeated several times before he was actually aware of it. He sat slowly up in his bunk and listened. It sounded like—it had to be—a puppy whimpering. Softly he called, "Gramp! I hear something that sounds like a puppy. Wake up and listen."

Cap'n Tony swung his feet over the side of his bunk and sat still. Sure enough, he heard it too. Quickly he pulled on his trousers, slipped his feet into shoes, picked up his flashlight, and started for the outside deck. Manuel was right behind him, and silently the two swung over the side of the boat. Following the noise, they tiptoed over the dock and up to the side of the warehouse at the end. As they neared the building the whimpering stopped, so they waited quietly until it started again. They were standing close to an old coil of line and several boxes piled up together. When the noise sounded again, Cap'n Tony stepped forward quickly to a box which was turned on its side.

He shone his flashlight around a time or two, then it stopped on the side-turned box. 'Way in the back, in the farthest corner, huddled a tiny black puppy! It was curled into a ball not much larger than Cap'n Tony's fist, and its eyes, shining yellow in the light, seemed to be the biggest thing about it.

Manuel reached in and picked up the little black ball. The puppy squeaked once, then settled down in

25

the boy's arms, and, except for his trembling, he seemed to be perfectly at home.

"Let's take him to the boat, Manuel," said gramp, "then we can see what we have in the way of a dog."

Back on the *Miss Abbie*, they discovered they had found a puppy who was solid black except for four white feet. He was fat and roly-poly and seemed to be in good condition, judging by the silkiness of his fur.

"Can we keep him, gramp?" asked Manuel excitedly. "I've always wanted a dog, and we found him, you know. Please let me keep him, gramp."

"Right now I think you'd better give him something to eat," replied gramp. "While you feed him, I'll fix him a bed for tonight. When he's finished eating, we'll all go to sleep, and we can talk about keeping him or not in the morning."

Even though he was fat as a butterball, the puppy greedily lapped the milk Manuel gave him. Then gramp put him into a box with an old towel in it and placed the box by the side of the second lower bunk.

"I think maybe you'd better sleep in this bunk for tonight, Manuel," he said. "Then when the puppy cries during the night, you can touch him and he'll go back to sleep."

Manuel was happy with this arrangement, and soon the lights were out and they were back in bed.

"Please have good dreams tonight, gramp," whispered Manuel, "so you'll wake up feeling fine tomor-

27

row and will let me keep this puppy. And you, little dog, sleep tight and be quiet tonight, and maybe tomorrow he'll say you can stay."

3.
Footsie's First Day

The next morning Manuel's eyes popped wide open as Cap'n Tony's feet hit the deck. For just a second he lay still, trying to think why he was so happy. Then he heard the puppy, grunting and nosing around in his box, and he remembered. A wide grin came over his face, and he picked up the dog and held him close. The pup stuck out his little pink tongue and licked Manuel's nose, and Manuel laughed and rumpled the silky black fur.

From the galley Cap'n Tony called, "You'd better come and fix breakfast for the dog while I get ours."

"Have you decided whether I can keep him or not, gramp?" inquired Manuel anxiously.

"I haven't made up my mind yet, Manuel," answered gramp. "We'll take him out with us today on a trial run, so to speak. When we get back tonight

29

and have more time, we'll see if anybody around here knows anything about whose he is or where he came from. I promise you I'll decide before we go to sleep tonight, but right now we must get ready for our day's work."

About the time the three finished breakfast Jerry came on board. Manuel jumped up and called, "Jerry, come see what I've got," and scooped the puppy up to show him to the striker.

"Gosh, isn't he cute!" said Jerry. "Where'd you get 'im?"

"We found him on the dock last night," replied Manuel, "and gramp hasn't decided yet whether I can keep him or not. We're going to take him out with us today, then ask around the dock tonight when we get back. If he behaves himself today and nobody claims him tonight, maybe, just maybe, gramp will let me keep him. Golly," he added wistfully, "I sure hope I can."

"Jerry," said Cap'n Tony, "if we're going to catch any shrimp today, we'd better get started. I don't believe we're going to have much help from Manuel," and his eyes twinkled as he turned away.

Manuel put the pup into his box just long enough to help Cap'n Tony and Jerry get the *Miss Abbie* underway. Then he went to the puppy in the cabin. He had curled up and gone back to sleep, and Manuel sat and watched him for a while. When the boat reached the shrimping grounds and the net was put over the side, Manuel picked up the box with the puppy in it and took it to the pilothouse. He set it down, and the pup stood up and put his paws on the side of the box. He looked inquiringly around him, then back at Manuel.

"If we keep him, gramp," said Manuel, "I've thought of a name for him. It's Footsie because of his four white feet."

"That's a good name all right," said gramp, "but don't get your heart set on him yet, Manuel, for I still haven't made up my mind."

"Oh, I haven't!" said Manuel quickly. And gramp smiled at the boy's quick denial.

The puppy tried to crawl out of the box, but at first he couldn't make it. He grunted and pushed and wiggled and struggled, but the sides were too high. Manuel said, "Here, Footsie. Here, Footsie, come here." Footsie was so mad because he couldn't get to Manuel that he sat down and yipped, then he fussed, and then he cried. Manuel kept calling, and Footsie kept trying, and by and by, out he came in a tumble. He rolled over, then stood up and staggered his way to Manuel. He crawled into the boy's lap as he sat cross-legged on the deck of the pilothouse and snuggled down to rest from his struggles.

When it was time for the net to be raised, Cap'n Tony told Manuel he had better put the box and the puppy in the cabin and shut him in there. "He'd just be in the way, and you'd have to watch him every second," said Cap'n Tony. "You surely would hate to have anything bad happen to him, and he's so little and wobbly that he can't control his movements yet. He's tired, anyhow, and needs to get a nap. Even though he's a dog, he's just a baby and needs a lot of sleep."

Manuel was so anxious to keep Footsie that he

32

jumped up quickly and did as gramp suggested. Then he went to the stern to help with the shrimp, but he kept thinking about Footsie all the time. As soon as everything had been stored or washed away, back to the cabin he went. He tiptoed to the box to look at the puppy, but the box was empty! Footsie was nowhere to be seen!

He looked everywhere in the cabin, but he couldn't find Footsie. He looked under the bunks, under the chest in the corner, behind the wastebasket by the chest—still no Footsie. Then the terrible thought came to him that maybe Footsie had gotten out of the cabin and fallen overboard! He closed the door of the cabin and raced to the pilothouse.

"Gramp!" he cried, "I can't find Footsie. I put him in his box in the cabin as you said, and when I went to get him just now, he was gone!"

"Now don't get excited, Manuel," said Cap'n Tony. "Are you sure the cabin door was closed?"

"Yes! At least I'm pretty sure it was," cried Manuel. "I think I closed it tight when I went to help you and Jerry. But Footsie isn't in his box, and I can't find him anywhere in the cabin. I've looked everywhere, and he's just not there. Oh, I do hope he hasn't fallen overboard. Please let Jerry steer and you come see if you can find him."

Jerry took the wheel, and Cap'n Tony and Manuel returned to the cabin. The door was closed, and they

33

went inside and looked in the box. Manuel felt that Footsie would just have to be there, but the box was still empty.

"Now don't get excited, son," said his granddad. "If the door was closed, he's got to be in here somewhere. Let's look carefully and we'll find him, I'm sure. Did you try calling him?"

"No," said Manuel. "I guess I was so scared I forgot. Here, Footsie, here. Here, Footsie, come here," he called, and his voice sounded as though he was about to cry. "Here, Foots—" and he stopped right in the middle of the call.

Out from under the pillow on Manuel's bunk scrambled Footsie! "How in the world did he get up there?" cried Manuel. "Footsie, how did you manage to get up on my bunk? Why did you hide from me?"

Cap'n Tony looked at the distance from the deck of the cabin to the top of the bunk and said, "It's just about as high as his box sides are, so he could have done it. But, Footsie, how did you do it?"

The puppy looked at Manuel and took one lick at his nose, but he didn't say a word. "I guess we'll never know how he did it," said Manuel.

Each time he left the cabin that day Manuel made sure that the door was closed. And he kept hoping that gramp wouldn't think Footsie was too much trouble to keep.

When they reached the dock that afternoon, Manuel

could hardly wait to visit the other boats and find out
if anyone could tell them about Footsie. But gramp
insisted that the chores be done and supper eaten before they set out. When Manuel finally felt that he
could stand it no longer, gramp said, "I believe we've
done all that needed doing now, Manuel, so we'll take
Footsie and do some checking."

They went from boat to boat, and though the captains admired Footsie, nobody had seen him before
or knew where he came from. Cap'n Joe, owner of
the *Mary Lou,* said, "If the boy wants the dog, Tony,
why don't you quit hunting an owner and let him
stay? I've had my dog Mike here, going on about three
years. I never knew where he came from. He never
told me and I never asked him. He's been with me so
long now he thinks he owns the boat, and we get along
just fine."

"I just hate to think that somebody has lost this
cute pup," said Cap'n Tony, "but we've asked all over
the dock. Since nobody claims him, Manuel, you may
keep Footsie."

"Thank you, gramp, thank you," said Manuel. "Oh,
I was so afraid you wouldn't let him stay. Then when
he was lost today, I was sure you would think he was
too much trouble!"

"It's going to be up to you to see that he's fed and
bathed and everything else, son. He's your dog now,
so you'll have to take care of him."

"I will," promised Manuel happily. "I'll teach him the most tricks any dog ever knew. He'll follow me everywhere I go, and he'll be the most beautiful dog you ever saw," he said as he hugged the little black mite to him.

"You're going to have to teach him a lot more things than tricks," said Cap'n Tony. "There's lots of things more important than lying down and rolling over. He's got to learn all about a boat and how to stay out of the way of the net—and us, too," he added. "You'll have to teach him where he can go on the boat and where he can't. He's going to have to learn not to get close to the side when the sea's rough or he'll fall overboard. He's going to have to get his sea legs so he can walk around even when the boat's moving. You'd better start on those things first, 'cause they're a lot more important than tricks."

"I'll do whatever you say, gramp," promised Manuel. "I've always wanted a dog, and I've always wanted to go to sea with you, and just think! I've got both my wishes at one time!"

Manuel put Footsie down on the dock, and Mike came up to inspect the pup. They sniffed each other over, then Mike put his stamp of approval on the newcomer by starting a game of chase. By the time they went to sleep that night, Footsie was acting as though he'd been on board the *Miss Abbie* all his short life. Manuel snuggled down in his bunk in a state of complete happiness.

36

4.
Stormy Picnic

Days passed and Footsie grew. He made a trip to the vet's to get his first distemper shot, then was taken to the dime store for his first ball. Manuel bought one with a bell in it, and Cap'n Tony said he could buy one more toy. After much picking and choosing, Manuel selected a little rubber pig and named it Porky. Each night Footsie put both toys in his bed, then curled around them to go to sleep.

By this time he began to get his sea legs and could walk all over the *Miss Abbie* even when the sea was rough. Once in a while, if he tried to run too fast, he would lose his balance, but most of the time he was quite steady.

One night when the boats were all tied up to the dock, Cap'n Joe and Mike came to visit on the *Miss Abbie*. Cap'n Joe said some of the men had been talking about taking off July 4 and having a big picnic.

They would take the wives, children, and dogs and go to the south end of Jekyll Island. All would go in small boats with outboard motors, and they could fish, swim, eat, and have a good time on the holiday. He said, "Tony, what do you think of this idea?"

Cap'n Tony replied, "Sounds like a good one. What do you think, Manuel? Would you and Footsie like to go on a picnic?"

Manuel yelled, "Yes, sir! I surely would. How 'bout you, Footsie?" And the puppy jumped up and started barking his answer.

"Then that's all settled," said Cap'n Joe. "The wives will make the lunches so you don't need to worry about food. We'll get an early start, and we can have the whole day to enjoy ourselves."

"Nobody would want the lunch I'd fix," said Cap'n Tony, "so we'll take a couple of cases of cold drinks. It's been a long time since I've been on a picnic like this, and it sounds like fun. I'm looking forward to it as much as Manuel is."

July 4 came, and everybody was happy to see that it was a good day for the picnic. The sun rose in a burst of glory, the air was nice and cool early that morning, and Manuel and Footsie were so excited they could hardly wait. Cap'n Tony iced the drinks in a big tub, and he and Cap'n Joe placed the tub in Cap'n Tony's little boat. All the boats were full of mamas, boys, girls, dogs, lunches, and lastly papas. All the outboard motors were finally started (though one gave a lot of trouble at first), and the party started out. They made quite a lot of noise as they moved down the river on the same route the men took every morning. The motors sounded like angry bees buzzing as loud as they could, and over this noise could be heard the children calling from boat to boat. And the dogs! Each one seemed to be trying to outbark the rest. It was all very exciting except it was too noisy to hear yourself think. But who wanted to think, anyhow!

When the first boat reached St. Simons Sound, it turned south into Jekyll Creek. All the others followed. After about fifteen minutes they reached the southern tip of Jekyll Island, which was their destination. It had a sandy beach, and behind this were lots of trees for shade during the hot part of the day. One by one the boats pulled up on the beach, and two by two the children and dogs hopped out into the shallow water. They raced up and down the island and into the water, splashing each other as they ran. The lunches and drinks were unloaded and taken up to the shade. The boats were anchored securely so they could not drift away down the creek, and everybody started enjoying themselves.

Some grown people fished, and the children swam, ran up and down the beach and in and out of the water, until all were starved. Then the mamas spread the lunch, and everybody gathered 'round. Cap'n

Tony was asked to say grace, and the group was silent for the first time that day. Even the dogs were quiet, sitting close to their masters with their eyes fastened on the food.

And what a feast that was! Fried chicken, baked ham, sliced roast beef, all kinds of salads and sandwiches, deviled eggs, and almost every kind of cake and pie you could mention! Everybody ate and ate until not a soul could possibly eat another bite and even the dogs quit begging. Everybody helped with the cleaning up. All the left-over lunch was packed, paper plates, napkins, and cups were burned, and all the bottles put back into the tub.

The children were then ready to go swimming again, but the mamas said, "No! Not for an hour, at least. After what you've eaten, you'd get cramps so fast you'd sink before anybody could get to you." So they sat down in the shade until time to go back into the water. It was good to sit for a while and rest, too, for all had been so busy they were tired out. Some of the men stretched out on the leaves and took little naps.

The hour passed quickly, and soon the beach was dotted again with swimmers and fishermen and fisherwomen. Just past the middle of the afternoon, Cap'n Tony noticed a dark cloud on the horizon. At first he didn't say anything about it, but he kept watching it. He knew that summer storms could blow up in a short time and bring high winds and rain. The cloud grew darker and rose quickly into the sky. Cap'n Tony pointed it out to several of the men, and they decided they had better leave the island. They didn't want the wind and rain to catch them out on the water.

The boats were loaded as quickly as possible, and one by one they left the island. Cap'n Tony helped each one to get away. The cloud kept moving closer and closer, the sun vanished, and the wind began to blow very hard. Screaming seagulls were flying with the wind, and the creek suddenly became full of waves with whitecaps.

By this time Cap'n Joe, with his wife and five children and Mike, and Cap'n Tony with Manuel and Footsie were the only ones left on Jekyll. Cap'n Joe's motor was started, but the wind and waves were strong, and he had such a heavy load that he couldn't leave. He made several attempts, and each time his boat was turned around and shoved back to land. The third time he tried, a huge wave broke over the little boat, nearly capsizing it and almost swamping it.

"Gramp!" shouted Manuel over the scream of the wind, "you had better take some of Cap'n Joe's children in your boat and leave Footsie and me here. There isn't room for all of us, and Footsie and I are big and strong and can take this little blow all right. You can come back for us after you get the others home safely."

"I believe the boy's right, Joe," called Cap'n Tony.

"You'll never get your little ones home all in one boat, and Manuel and Footsie can get under the trees and wait. As soon as we deliver your family, I'll return for them."

Cap'n Joe protested some, but in his heart he knew what Manuel and gramp said was true, and there wasn't time to argue. Quickly Mrs. Joe and two of her children were transferred to Cap'n Tony's boat, and both boats were able to leave immediately.

"Go back under the trees, Manuel, and wait there for me. I'll be back in a short time, I hope," instructed gramp.

As soon as Manuel saw the boats leave safely, he and Footsie scampered to the trees, but they were not much protection against the weather. The wind was blowing the rain so hard it felt like needles stinging his skin, and he began to shiver with cold. He selected the largest tree he could find and crouched against it on the leeward side, away from the wind. He took Footsie in his lap and leaned over the pup in order to shield him as much as possible, and both waited, wet and cold, in the howling, shrieking grayness.

Suddenly Manuel heard a frightening new noise. He looked up just in time to see a huge limb tear loose from a nearby tree and come hurtling toward him and Footsie. He flung the puppy to one side and jumped to cover him, but he did not get completely clear. One end of the limb caught him with a glancing blow, and he fell, unconscious.

The next thing he knew, Footsie was licking his face, and two strange men in oilskins were standing over him.

"We're coastguardsmen from the station on St. Simons," explained one. "Are you hurt bad, son?"

"No. I don't think so," answered Manuel, feeling his shoulder. "A big limb fell and hit me as I was trying to get Footsie and me out of its way. But how did you know where I was?"

"Your grandfather called and told us to come get you. The storm is too bad for him to get back so he told us where you were. When we reached the island

and started ashore to hunt for you, your pup came running down to the beach. He must've heard us, for he met us and brought us straight here to you. Now let's get back to our boat so you can change those wet clothes and get some hot coffee before you take your death of cold. Can you walk?"

Manuel scrambled painfully to his feet but said scornfully, "Sure, I can walk. That was just a little bump," and the four made their way to the beach.

They climbed into a small boat, and one of the men started the motor. It took them only a few minutes to reach the larger boat which could not come into shallow water. They boarded it, and one of the men secured the small boat at its stern. Then they started for home. Manuel rubbed himself dry with a big, rough towel and put on the men's clothes that were given him. He dried Footsie on the towel as he sipped hot coffee, and soon they both stopped shivering from the cold. Footsie was given a bowl of coffee, too, and he lapped it as fast as he could.

Manuel felt very important when the big coastguard boat pulled up alongside the *Miss Abbie,* and Cap'n Tony was at the rail waiting for him.

"The boy saved the dog's life, and the dog returned the favor," called one of the coastguardsmen. "Get Manuel to tell you all about it. We'll pick up our clothes some other time. Got to get back to the station in case somebody else needs help," and the boat roared away down the river.

Manuel told Cap'n Tony the whole story. He was very proud of Footsie, and Cap'n Tony was even prouder of Manuel, but all were tired and went to bed earlier than usual. The storm lasted until midnight when it blew itself out. But the wind and waves didn't trouble anyone on board the *Miss Abbie*. All three slept, snug and sound, and the next morning the adventure seemed like a bad dream.

5.

Adventure with an Eagle

Cap'n Tony pressed the starter button, and the motor began humming instantly. He stood quietly, listening to the even purring of the big diesel engine. Then he called, "O.K., Manuel. Cast off."

Manuel was waiting by the piling on the dock for these words. He knew exactly what to do now, even in the pitch-black darkness. Quickly he loosened the line from the piling and tossed it to the deck of the shrimper, jumping aboard at almost the same second. He coiled the loose line neatly on the pile already there and walked forward to join his grandfather and Jerry in the pilothouse. Not a word was spoken as Cap'n Tony maneuvered the boat away from the dock and headed out into the river, but Footsie did enough talking for all of them.

Footsie loved these early morning take-offs. Almost

every shrimp boat had a dog aboard, and each one felt his own importance as the boats left for the day's fishing. Footsie seemed to feel that his barking was the fuel that made the boat keep running. He was as quiet as a mouse until the motor started. That was his signal to start barking, and he barked constantly as the boats made their unerring way down the river toward the sound. His eyes glowed now with excitement, and his feathery tail stood straight out behind him in the sea breeze. Little drops of moisture formed on his muzzle from the damp air, but these worried him none as he urged the boat ahead with his barking.

Miss Abbie's motor purred, and so did the motors of the other boats in the shrimp fleet as all the boats made their way out to the deep shrimping waters. Everything that needed to be done had been taken care of on time. The net had been checked the afternoon before to be sure there were no holes through which the shrimp could escape. Ice had been loaded into the hold to keep the catch fresh on the return trip. Fuel had been pumped into the tanks to keep the motor running, and there were groceries aplenty in the little refrigerator in the galley. The stars overhead were shining brightly, and there was very little wind—not enough to cause many waves that day. All were happy and at peace with the world, each with his own thoughts.

Cap'n Tony was thinking what a good life he had

—working at something he knew and loved—with his grandson by his side, learning the business and loving it as he did. Jerry was thinking that today was payday and he could take his girl to the movie that night. Manuel was happy in his thoughts, too. He was remembering Footsie the first time he had seen him—a little, tiny black ball of fur with great, golden eyes shining into the flashlight, huddled in the back corner of the box on the dock. And Footsie was thinking who knew what? Perhaps he was hoping they would catch another big blue crab with no claws and he could play with it as he had done the other day.

The sky was turning pink, and the seagulls had started out to look for their breakfasts when the *Miss Abbie* reached the shrimping waters. The motor was slowed, and Jerry and Manuel were busy putting the net overboard to make their first drag of the day. Footsie was very careful to stay out of their way. Being a seafaring dog, he learned first of all that he must not get in the way as the net went overboard or he would be caught by it and go overboard, too.

This job was done quickly because striker and helper had done it so many times before they knew exactly how to go about their business. Then the four settled down for a smooth slow ride around the sound while the net did the work. The other members of the shrimp fleet either had their nets out or were putting them, and the day's trawling had started.

48

Cap'n Tony turned on the radio to get the early morning broadcast of the news. They heard this report, which was followed by the weather forecast for the day. When this was over, Cap'n Tony turned off the radio, and Manuel went on deck. He looked for Footsie and spied him standing at the stern, watching the water bubble up from the propeller. As Manuel stood there watching his little pet, from out of the blue sky plunged a huge bird—straight for the boat!

At first Manuel was so startled he could hardly sense what was happening. Then he realized that this bird was a bald eagle and he was headed straight for Footsie. The speed of the bird was so swift that before Manuel could move or even shout, the eagle had swooped upon Footsie, snatched him up in his talons, and darted skyward with the little dog!

Footsie was screaming with all his might. This crying was completely different from the bragging barking he had done on the way out to sea. He was terrified. All the world he had known in his short lifetime had held nothing like this for him. The eagle's claws were digging into his ribs, and he couldn't get his breath. He was being taken higher and higher into the air, and his beloved master and home were going farther and farther away each moment.

For Manuel, the world seemed to stop for a few seconds as the eagle snatched Footsie from the stern of the boat and soared off. He was so horrified he could

only stand and watch the two as the distance widened between them and the boat. When he finally heard Footsie's pitiful cries, he jumped as though he had been shocked by an electric wire. He raced into the pilothouse, calling to gramp what had just happened.

Without a word, Jerry jumped to take the wheel while gramp snatched the rifle from its rack and raced on deck. Breathing a small prayer of thanks that the sea was so calm and the boat so still, he took very careful aim and fired.

A small puff of feathers flew from the eagle, and Manuel knew gramp had hit the bird and not Footsie, but had the eagle been wounded enough to stop him? He watched so hard his eyes ached and tears ran down his cheeks. And just then he saw the big bird start to spiral downward, still grasping Footsie in his talons.

Jerry turned the boat toward the spot where the eagle was drifting from the sky, and the boat and bird were soon very close together. Manuel ran to the side of the boat and grabbed up a long-handled dip net lashed to it. Just as the eagle's wing tips touched the surface of the water, Footsie saw his master and made a terrific lunge toward him. The eagle's grip relaxed, and Footsie was free. Manuel scooped him up with the net, and once again the little fellow was in his own little dog heaven—his master's arms.

For a few seconds Manuel could do nothing but stand hugging Footsie, and both shook all over with

51

terror and relief. Then Manuel took his small cargo to the pilothouse where he and Cap'n Tony looked the little dog over for wounds. Iodine from the first-aid kit was carefully swabbed into every scratch, and, though Footsie winced from the burning, he continued to lick Manuel's face and hands just as hard as he could.

For the rest of the day Footsie lay curled up in his bed in a corner of the pilothouse. He was stiff and sore and was content to lie still and sleep or watch Manuel as he went about his duties.

But when the last drag was made and the last shrimp put in ice and the boat turned up the river toward the dock, Footsie raised his head and looked around him. He stood up and saw the other boats around him all heading toward home, with their various dogs standing proudly by their masters.

Then he started barking as he had never barked before. Who knows but he was telling his dog friends of the experience of the day, for every single dog on every single boat was as quiet as quiet could be— listening to Footsie's tale?

6.
Whitey and Ditto

As the *Miss Abbie* moved down the Brunswick River toward St. Simons Sound, Footsie stood as far forward in the bow as he could. The water slipping smoothly backward seemed to fascinate him so much that he forgot his usual barking and stood there watching intently. Suddenly he spied a dark shape heading toward the *Miss Abbie*'s bow from the water beyond. He had never seen anything like this before.

The large dark shape came right up to the side of the boat, then instead of bumping into it, turned and went right along with it. Footsie couldn't understand this at all. The thing was going at exactly the same speed as the boat, side by side with it, and yet it didn't make a sound. Sometimes it was quite deep in the water, and Footsie leaned over as far as he dared, trying to see whether it was still there or if it had gone. Then it would rise close to the surface and continue its gliding, just barely a few inches underneath the water.

Footsie watched and wondered as long as he could. He turned his head down on one side and then on the other, still trying to decide what the shape was. Finally he could stand it no longer. He yipped a sharp bark and waited to see what happened. Nothing did. He gave another and another, and still the thing continued to move along with the boat, never faster, never slower, just gliding along up and down.

Now Footsie had never been ignored in all his short life. Other dogs sniffed or growled or barked at him. People said, "Ooooh and aaaah" and "Isn't he darling" and "What's his name?" and all sorts of silly noises that people make when they see a solid black puppy with four white feet and eyes as bright as shiny marbles. But until now, he had never been completely ignored. And he didn't like it at all.

His barking grew louder and more shrill until Manuel came around the deck from the pilothouse to investigate Footsie's actions. Manuel went up to the little dog and leaned over the side of the boat to see what was making Footsie bark so loud. Then he laughed and laughed. Cap'n Tony called out, "What is it, Manuel?"

"It's only a porpoise, gramp. Footsie has never seen one before, and he can't understand how it can swim

54

right along with the boat. I think the fact that the porpoise isn't barking or talking to him makes him mad. Anyhow, that's all it is."

Manuel turned and went back to his granddad, and Footsie, satisfied that the thing couldn't harm him, turned and trotted along with the boy.

Many times that day Footsie left his master and went to the bow of the boat to look over the side. Each time, the porpoise was still in its same place, and Footsie became so used to it that he no longer barked or seemed upset at being ignored. When the shrimp net was lowered for the many drags they made that day, the porpoise left the side of the boat and trailed behind the net. Cap'n Tony and Manuel knew it was feeding on the shrimp which had been fast enough to escape being caught in the net, but they were surprised that the big porpoise stayed with them so long. Secretly, each was pleased that this was happening, for every shrimper knows it's good luck for a porpoise to follow a boat. Sure enough, the catch that day was the most of any day that season, and the shrimp were larger. That meant a bigger check in the bank for gramp, and they were happy.

As the *Miss Abbie* started toward home port, the porpoise came close to the side again, sprang into the air, and blew a farewell spout of water before disappearing toward the ocean. As it did this, Manuel and Cap'n Tony noticed a large white spot right by the

55

blow-hole in its head. This was very unusual, for porpoises are usually gray all over and have no distinguishing color markings.

"Good-by, Whitey," called Manuel to the disappearing porpoise. "Thanks for a good catch, and come back with us fishing again soon."

That evening back at the dock, Cap'n Tony and Manuel were comparing catches with the other shrimpers. The others had done well but the *Miss Abbie* had beaten them all. Manuel wondered if Whitey was really the cause of their good luck that day.

The next morning Manuel was out on the bow with Footsie as the sun rose. Both were waiting to see if Whitey would join them for that day's fishing. Sure enough, when they reached a certain oyster reef in the sound, the same dark shape darted toward the boat, and Whitey joined them again. They had good luck again that day, and when they started up the river toward home, Whitey jumped into the air and told them goodnight with the usual big splash of water. The sun seemed to shine on the white spot even more brightly than the day before.

Whitey continued to join the *Miss Abbie* day after day, and the shrimping continued to be good. This was the best season the *Miss Abbie* ever had.

But one morning Whitey didn't appear when they reached the reef. All day long Manuel and Footsie watched and waited, and even Footsie seemed to feel that something was wrong. The usual seagulls were there, staying behind the boat while it trawled, then swarming up close when they saw the net hauled in. They screamed and dipped and dived, fighting each other for the tiny fish Manuel and Jerry threw over the side, but they still did not take the place of the familiar Whitey.

The next day was the same. Whitey didn't appear, and Manuel and Footsie missed the big porpoise very much. The catch was still good, however, and Cap'n Tony wondered if Whitey's luck was with them even though Whitey wasn't.

For several days things went on in the same way, and Manuel stopped talking about Whitey. He often found himself looking for Whitey, however, and hoped that one day they would see the big porpoise again.

One morning Footsie wandered to his usual place in the bow of the *Miss Abbie* and looked down over the side to watch the water slipping by. As he looked, a familiar dark shape came darting toward the boat, but this time it wasn't alone. Right by the side of it was another one, shaped just like the first, swimming just like the first, but, oh, so much smaller. Now Footsie had become used to the first big shape, but this was something different—a big shape and a little shape, both swimming side by side right along with the boat. He gave a sharp yip, and Manuel looked toward him. Footsie yipped again and again and looked first at Manuel then over the side of the boat as though saying, "Come see what I've found this time."

Manuel hoped it would be Whitey who had returned to join them, but he didn't really believe it would be. To satisfy Footsie, however, he walked out to the puppy and sure enough, there was Whitey again. Then he spied the small object beside Whitey, and suddenly Whitey's disappearance was explained. He turned and ran back to the pilothouse and Cap'n Tony.

"Gramp," he called, "Whitey is back with us again, and guess what! She has her baby with her!"

"Bless my soul!" choked Cap'n Tony. "Jerry, hold the wheel while I go take a look."

Jerry took the wheel, and Cap'n Tony hurried to the bow to speak to Whitey and her baby. Whitey seemed to know she was the center of attraction and also seemed to enjoy it. She gave a leap into the air— not a very high leap this time, though—and the baby swam as close to the surface of the water as it could to be near its mother. And right by the blow-hole of the baby porpoise was a tiny white spot!

When Cap'n Tony returned to the pilothouse, Manuel was trying to decide on a name for the baby. When he learned of the baby's white spot he said, "Well! That makes naming him much easier. We'll call him Ditto."

Going home that afternoon Manuel said, "Gramp,

do you think I've been aboard long enough now to try steering? I've watched you so much; it's daylight and not night! There's not much wind blowing, and there are no other boats real close to us. Will you let me try, please?"

He said this all in such a rush that gramp had to laugh at him. "I'm glad you didn't run out of breath that time, Manuel," he said. "I thought sure you'd turn blue in the face before you finished, but you didn't miss a word. You'll never be satisfied until you steer, and what you say is true, so you may take the wheel now. Just be sure to watch the buoys. Line them up as I have shown you, and you'll stay in the channel."

Manuel's heart was beating so hard he was afraid gramp would notice, but if he did, he didn't say anything. The boy wasn't quite tall enough so gramp put a box for him to stand on, and Manuel grasped the spokes of the big wheel. He tried very hard to do exactly as Gramp did, but every time he turned the wheel it went too far. The line of foam behind the boat looked like jagged lightning, 'way out to the right, then to the left, then to the right, and back again. Manuel was so provoked he could have cried; it looked so easy when gramp did it!

Finally gramp took the wheel and said, "You've done very well for your first time, Manuel, much better than Jerry did on his first try, hasn't he, Jerry?"

Jerry looked at gramp sheepishly and said, "He sure did, Cap'n Tony. You remember, I nearly ran us on a sand bar, and you had to grab the wheel from me in a hurry to save us!"

That made Manuel feel a little better, but not much. Before the summer was over, would he be able to take the *Miss Abbie* up the river and dock her?

7.
Whitey and the Shark

This morning when Manuel waked, Cap'n Tony was just taking breakfast off the little gas stove, so they sat down to eat. Footsie took his usual place at Manuel's knee and started his little rumbling noises to remind Manuel that he was there and hungry, too, and wanted his tidbits from the meal. Manuel gave him little bits of bacon, and Footsie was silent until he thought he was forgotten. Then he rumbled again, and Manuel gave him a little egg on a bit of toast.

As the boat made her way down the river, Manuel could tell it was going to be a beautiful day by the brightness of the stars overhead, by the little breeze that tickled his ears, and by the tiny fingers of light that showed it would not be very long before the sun would be peeping over the big Atlantic Ocean ahead of them.

When the *Miss Abbie* reached a certain reef, the sun had risen, and Manuel and Footsie were at their usual places on the bow, waiting for Whitey and Ditto to appear. Soon the mama porpoise and her baby came darting from the depths and started swimming along with the boat. These two and Footsie had become such good friends now that when they came up to the boat, Footsie barked only once as though saying, "Good morning! Now we can get to our business, for we are all here."

When Cap'n Tony decided it was time to put the shrimp net over, Manuel left Footsie and went aft to help Jerry. It went over the side with a splash, then the rope slithered out foot by foot until it was right behind the boat. This meant the net had gone as far as it could and the boards had spread out in order to open the net wide so it could catch many shrimp. Manuel then went to the pilothouse to join his grandad. They listened to the radio until Cap'n Tony thought it was time to haul in the net for their first catch of the day.

Manuel pressed the button that caused the winch to haul in the net, and in it came, very slowly. This seemed to be the signal that called the seagulls to the side of the *Miss Abbie*. Nobody knows how gulls can tell when it's time to gather around a shrimp boat, but when a net is hauled in, they start collecting.

Footsie stayed out of the way very carefully while

all this was going on. Manuel had explained to him that a seafaring dog helps his master by not getting in the way. He also helps himself by not getting caught in the net and being dragged overboard! Whitey and Ditto had followed the net while it was trawling and now were swimming lazily around, waiting for the boat to start dragging again before they took their places by the bow.

The gulls circled and darted over the boat. Sometimes they flew so low it seemed as if they were saying, "Hurry up with our breakfasts. Can't you see we're starving? You're so slow. Why can't you work faster?" Indeed they were screeching at the tops of their lungs, so impatient were they for food. One special gull darted right at Footsie just as though he were trying to get Footsie to help so they could eat sooner. It came so close to the puppy that he jumped up to catch it, but quick as a flash the bird flew skyward. Whether it was this same bird or another nobody knew, but one flew too close to Footsie again. The pup chased it to the side of the boat, and as the bird zipped up over the side and out of the way, Footsie jumped, lost his balance, and over the side he went!

His little black head popped to the surface immediately, but he didn't look like the same pup who had chased the gull to the side of the boat. His silky black hair was soaking wet and plastered to his head, and his long feathery tail trailed out behind as he paddled

63

lazily around the warm ocean. His big shiny eyes were
the same, however, and he kept them fastened on
Manuel as the boy continued to work with the shrimp.
It took Footsie a few seconds to realize that his master
didn't know he had gone overboard. Then he decided
he'd better tell Manuel what had happened, so he
opened his wet mouth and yipped.

When Manuel heard Footsie's bark, his head nearly

flew off his neck as he jerked around to see the little dog in the water. Then his eyes nearly popped out of his head, for just beyond the wet black head of his puppy he saw the fin of a shark. It seemed like hours that he stood there, watching the fin move closer and closer to the helpless little dog.

Suddenly, there was a terrific splash and the water started churning around the shark. The shark's fin disappeared beneath the surface of the water, and great bubbles rose to the top. The water was whirling and churning so, it looked like a giant kettle was underneath, boiling and bubbling. Though time seemed to stand still, it could have been only a few seconds before Manuel realized what had happened. In circling around the *Miss Abbie*, Whitey had seen the shark and attacked it. Porpoises hate all sharks and will attack and kill them whenever possible.

Manuel watched the battle as well as he could. First the shark and the porpoise were both hidden from sight, deep under the water. Then the shark leaped high into the air, trying to escape his enemy. Both dived beneath the surface, and blood from the shark rose to the surface. Then the shark was tossed high into the air again.

During this time Footsie was still paddling around in the water, unaware that one mighty fish was fighting another to the death to save his own little life. He wondered why Manuel didn't dip him up in the net as he had done before when Footsie went overboard, but he wasn't worried. Hadn't he always been rescued?

Finally the shark was thrown high into the air for the last time. When he hit the surface of the ocean, he didn't swim, but sank slowly down, down.

When he disappeared from sight and Manuel realized that Whitey had really killed him, it seemed as though something that had been holding Manuel snapped, and he jumped for the side of the boat. With a sigh of relief he spied Footsie, still paddling around in circles as close to the boat as he could get. From the side of the boat came the trusty old dip net, and Footsie was once again on the deck of the *Miss Abbie*.

He shook himself all over, getting as much water on Manuel as he shook off himself. Then he looked reproachfully at Manuel with his sorrowful eyes. The boy could almost hear Footsie think, "Well, it's time you brought me back on board. I know I did wrong to fall overboard, but you didn't have to punish me by making me stay in the water such a long time."

Trouble and Footsie seemed made for each other.

8.
Footsie Guards the Boat

It had been a good day for everybody on the *Miss Abbie*. For once, Footsie stayed out of trouble. As usual, his bed was placed in the pilothouse so he could nap in it when he felt sleepy. When the net was out and things were dull for Footsie, he had gone to his bed several times during the day and had taken little naps, so he felt rested and very wide awake.

He always woke up when it was time to take in the net and sort out the shrimp, however, so he was on hand to see something funny. Manuel and Jerry were separating the shrimp from the net and putting them on the deck to head. Suddenly Manuel touched a large squid in the net. A second name for squid is ink-fish, for it secretes a black liquid in its body. When a large fish comes near and the squid feels the fish is about to grab him to eat, it shoots out the ink. The water gets all cloudy and the squid darts away from its enemy. This particular squid had been caught in the net and hauled up on deck. When Manuel's hand touched it as he bent over, the squid acted as he did in the water. Out came a large inky squirt, and it landed right on Manuel's face! Jerry happened to be looking at Manuel when this happened, and he laughed and laughed. At first Manuel didn't think it was so funny. To have black liquid squirted all over his face was nothing to laugh at. But Jerry had him go to the cabin and look at himself in the mirror. When he saw the black streaks running down his face and dropping off his chin, he burst out laughing, too. He washed his face and went back on deck to finish sorting the shrimp, and he and Jerry chuckled together.

Footsie didn't know what had happened, but he could tell his two friends were happy. He wagged his tail and barked once or twice, trying to pretend he knew what had occurred and what they were laughing about, and he too thought it was funny. Whitey and Ditto just swam around the boat not knowing or caring what had happened. All they wanted was the boat to start moving again so they could get back of the net and catch shrimp.

There was a movie on at the theater that Manuel wanted very much to see. He finally talked Cap'n Tony into going, and they were in a hurry to finish the day's work so they could start back to the dock.

Manuel was excited, and the trip up the river seemed
as though it would never end. He always played with
Footsie on the way home and was teaching him some
fine tricks. Already he had taught him to sit up, shake
hands, roll over, lie down, and play dead. He worked
on these tricks now, and it made the time pass more
quickly.

They finally reached the dock, and Cap'n Tony
took the shrimp to the man who bought them. The
boat had been washed down and made ready for the
next day's trawling, ice was loaded into the hold, and
Manuel and Cap'n Tony took their showers. Cap'n
Tony cooked their supper in the galley, smoking his
pipe all the while. They ate in a hurry, and Manuel
fed Footsie.

While Footsie was eating his supper, Manuel explained to him that he and Cap'n Tony were going
ashore, but he couldn't go with them. He said little
dogs were not allowed to go to movies, and even if they
were, Footsie wouldn't have a good time. There was

nothing to do but sit still in the dark and look at pictures. There would be no birds to chase, no big blue crabs to play with, and no porpoises to bark at. He would be bored and would do nothing but sleep. He was going to be left on board the boat, but he was going to be in charge of the *Miss Abbie* and must look after her and see that nothing happened while they were gone. Footsie listened intently, turning his head down first one way and then the other, and he acted as though he understood every word Manuel said to him.

Cap'n Tony took a last puff on his pipe, laid it in the ash tray on the chest in the cabin, and came out on deck. He and Manuel waved good-by to Footsie, and off they went.

At first Footsie felt very important, being left in charge of the boat. He strutted around the deck so all the other dogs on the other boats tied up at the dock could see him. Just to be sure that nobody missed seeing him, he barked a few times. Soon, however, this became tiresome. He sat down on the deck and watched the few birds that were flying home. He began to feel sorry for himself, left all alone on this big boat. He howled a time or two but this made him feel silly—all those funny noises coming from him—so he decided he would go to bed and take a nap. Nobody would try to come aboard so there was really no need for him to sit up to guard the boat.

He went to his bed which had been put in the cabin for the night, and stepped into it. He turned around several times, pawed his mattress until he got it just right, then lay down and closed his eyes.

He had slept so much during the day, though, that he really wasn't sleepy now. He lay perfectly still waiting to go to sleep, when suddenly he smelled something. It was a smell different from any he knew, and he didn't like it. He raised his head and sniffed so hard his little black nose wiggled from side to side. He couldn't decide what this odor was, so he stepped out of his bed and started walking around the cabin, still sniffing.

As he walked toward the chest, the smell became stronger. A passing boat had made a wave which rocked the *Miss Abbie* more than usual. Cap'n Tony's pipe, full of hot ashes, had tumbled out of the ash tray and fallen into the papers in the wastebasket. He looked in that direction, and as he did, flames shot up from the wastebasket by the side of the chest! This was too much for Footsie, and he turned and ran out on deck. He was frightened and lonely, and he knew something was terribly wrong, so he barked.

Nobody paid any attention to him, and when Footsie realized that no help was coming, he scurried back into the cabin hoping the flames and the bad smell had gone away. Instead, however, they were worse. The flames were still there, only bigger, and now there was smoke which burned his eyes and nose. He ran back on deck again, and this time he really barked. He barked so fast that the barks tumbled over each other in his throat, trying to get out. This startled the other dogs, and they started barking too, and soon the whole dock was in an uproar.

The owners of the other dogs tried to make them hush their barking, but the dogs paid no attention. The men looked around and saw Footsie running frantically up and down the *Miss Abbie*'s deck, barking and barking, so they decided one of them should go aboard and see what was wrong.

The captain of the next boat jumped aboard the *Miss Abbie* and went inside to see what was making Footsie act so strangely. Instantly he saw what had caused the trouble. He ran out on deck, grabbed a bucket, scooped up water, and ran back to throw it on the fire. Twice more he threw buckets of water on the smoldering wastebasket. Then the fire was out, and there was nothing left but white smoke curling up from the blackened wastebasket. He looked around to make sure there was no more fire, then put the bucket in its place and returned to his own boat.

When Cap'n Tony and Manuel came home from the movie, Footsie was waiting for them as they swung on board. He barked to show them he was on the job, and this told the captain of the next boat the owner had returned. He came out on the deck of his boat and called out, "You sure do have a good dog."

"Thank you," said Manuel, "you have a good dog, too."

"Yes," said the man, "but not as good as yours. Look in your cabin, and you'll see what I mean."

Cap'n Tony and Manuel stepped curiously inside the cabin and turned on the light. When they saw the wet deck and the blackened wastebasket, they went back on deck. "What happened?" asked Cap'n Tony.

The captain told them how Footsie discovered the fire and barked until he made someone come put it out. All three praised Footsie and told him how smart he was to take such good care of the *Miss Abbie*.

Footsie knew this, and by now he was beginning to get very sleepy. It was 'way past his bedtime so he crawled into his bed, pawed the mattress once or twice just to be sure it was like he wanted it, then curled up and went sound asleep.

Maybe the excitement was over for good.

9.
Rescue at Sea

Manuel was teaching Footsie a wonderful new trick.
He and the little dog faced each other, Manuel sitting
flat on the deck and Footsie sitting on his little black
haunches. Manuel put his hands together and placed
them on his right cheek and bent his head to that side.
Then he brought them in front of his face and moved
them to his left cheek and bent his head in that direction. He had worked with Footsie on this special trick
many times during the past few days, and Footsie was
beginning to understand Manuel. He started doing
exactly as Manuel did, and once he did the trick perfectly. His big golden eyes watched Manuel intently,
for he was anxious to please his master.

Suddenly his eyes left Manuel's face, and he looked
out at the ocean. He had seen something. Manuel had
not seen it because his back was toward the direction
that Footsie was facing. The sun was not yet up, but

there was light enough for Footsie to see something floating in the water on the port side of the *Miss Abbie*. Now in the past few weeks he had seen many strange things, but never had he seen anything like this before.

He jumped up, leaving Manuel sitting on deck, and ran to the side of the boat. He stood with his white paws on the side of the boat, staring intently out over the Atlantic. When Manuel realized that Footsie had spied something, he went to see what it was. Imagine his surprise when he saw two people out there!

Quickly he ran to the pilothouse to tell gramp. Jerry took the wheel while Cap'n Tony picked up his bin-

oculars and went out on deck to see if what Manuel said was really true. Sure enough, through the powerful binoculars he saw a man and a woman out in the ocean. They both had on life jackets, and the man was waving his arms.

He sprang back into the pilothouse, turned his wheel hard to port, and started toward the floating man and woman. When he had the boat headed in the right direction, he held the wheel with one hand and reached for the ship-to-shore telephone with the other.

"KZYK," he shouted into the phone, "this is KZYW. KZYK, this is KZYW. Come in KZYK."

As he released the button, instantly he heard, "KZYW, this is KZYK. What's your trouble, Tony?"

"KZYK, this is KZYW. I've sighted a man and a woman floating in the water out here." Then he gave his location. "They are both alive—have on life jackets. I'm on my way to pick them up. Don't know whether they're hurt. In fact, don't know anything about them. Better have an ambulance go over to St. Simons Island, and we'll meet it there. I'll keep in touch if I need to, but you'd better hurry. Over."

He released the button again and heard the voice on shore say, "Ambulance will be crossing the causeway to St. Simons in two minutes. It'll be waiting at the end of the pier when you get there. If you need me, call again. Out."

In a matter of minutes the *Miss Abbie* reached the

couple in the water, and Manuel, Jerry, and Cap'n Tony hauled them shivering aboard the boat. Cap'n Tony then pushed the throttle to full speed ahead and raced toward St. Simons Island. Before the couple finished drinking the coffee Manuel made for them, they reached the pier. The ambulance attendants hustled them into the machine and off it roared, siren screaming.

Early-morning fishermen on the pier had gathered around the ambulance, asking questions of the attendants. Cap'n Tony told them briefly what he knew, then turned the *Miss Abbie* back toward the shrimping grounds, for he had work to do.

After supper that evening, Cap'n Tony, Manuel, and Footsie went to the hospital to see how their survivors were. Footsie had to wait in the car, but it was parked where he could be seen from the hospital windows. The couple felt fine, but the doctor wanted to keep them until the next day. He was afraid they might take pneumonia after being in the water so long.

"Have seats and visit with us a while," said the man. "We are the Taylors—Linda and Tom. We were flying to North Carolina to pick up our Tommy, who has been there in camp for a month. We planned to refuel at McKinnon Airport on St. Simons, but we ran into such strong head winds on the trip that we used more gas than we had counted on and went down in the water about two hours before you found us. We were floating there and could hear the other shrimp boats passing by, but it was too dark for them to see us. We called, but they couldn't hear us, either. We were wondering just how much longer we were going to have to stay there until somebody found us when you came along and saw us. It was bad enough being in the water at night, but I was afraid the sun would blister us during the day. We surely are grateful to you for noticing us and picking us up."

Manuel was sitting in a very straight chair, not saying a word. Cap'n Tony smiled at Mr. Taylor, then crooking his finger, he walked over to the window and motioned toward his car.

"There's the one who found you," he said, pointing toward Footsie. "If it hadn't been for that pup there, you might still be in the ocean. Manuel was teaching him a trick, and the pup was sitting on deck facing the direction where you were. He spied you and hopped up and ran to the side of the boat. He's the one who pointed you out to us, so you can thank him!"

When the *Miss Abbie* docked the next afternoon, who should be waiting there but Mr. and Mrs. Taylor. They had come to say good-by, and in their hands were four packages. Cap'n Tony's, Manuel's, and Jerry's had beautiful shirts, and Footsie's had a bright red collar. Manuel stooped over to fasten the collar around Footsie's neck, and he saw the tag had some writing on it. He held it up to read, and on the silver tag were engraved these words, "Footsie with grateful thanks from the Taylors."

Manuel's eyes glowed with pride as he fastened the gay collar around the neck of his little black dog. "Thank you very much from both of us," he said happily. "This is something good Footsie has done for a change. Maybe he and Trouble have finally parted company."

10.
Dognapers at Work

As the *Miss Abbie* pulled up to the dock from the day's shrimping, Manuel noticed a boy about his age walking around with a man and woman who looked like his parents. The three seemed to be tourists looking at the boats in the shrimp fleet. This was not unusual, for many strangers visited there.

Manuel jumped to the dock, taking with him the line from the boat in order to secure the *Miss Abbie* for the night. The new boy edged over to Manuel and asked if that was his boat. Manuel answered that it was his granddad's, and they both worked on it. About that time the boy noticed Footsie and asked, "Is that your dog?"

"Yes," said Manuel.

"What's his name?" inquired the newcomer.

"Footsie," replied Manuel.

"Does he know any tricks?" said the boy.

"Gosh, yes," replied Manuel, "lots of 'em."

"Make him do some," invited the boy.

Manuel was happy to show off his little pal to the visitor, so he jumped on to the boat, picked Footsie up in his arms, and jumped back on the dock. He had Footsie sit up, then lie down and play dead. He had him sit on his haunches and shake hands. Then he tried him on his newest trick—that of putting his paws together and placing them first on one side of his head and then on the other. Footsie seemed to know he was the center of admiring looks, and he performed every one of his tricks without a mistake.

The boy's mother and father came over to watch Footsie, and when he finished, all three clapped their hands. Footsie seemed to be laughing with them, for his mouth was wide open and his little pink tongue showed between his white, white teeth. The new boy said, "Oh, I want that dog. Dad, please buy him for me."

"How much will you take for him, son?" the father asked Manuel.

"He's not for sale," replied Manuel.

"Would you take twenty-five dollars for the dog?" asked the father.

"No," answered Manuel politely, "he's not for sale."

"What about fifty dollars?" asked the man.

Cap'n Tony came on deck and watched and listened

as the man went from fifty dollars to seventy-five dollars and finally offered one hundred dollars to Manuel. Each time Manuel told the man that Footsie was not for sale, that he wouldn't sell him for anything. And the visiting boy kept asking his dad to offer more money because he wanted the puppy more than anything in the world.

Finally Cap'n Tony said, "Seems to me by now you could see the boy isn't going to sell the dog and would let him alone. Money doesn't mean a thing to a boy, 'specially when it means swapping it for his pal. I'm glad he feels that way, 'cause I like the little dog, too. He's lots of company even if he is trouble at times. The boy isn't going to sell his dog, mister, so you may as well forget it and look for another dog for your son."

The man saw there was no use arguing further. Then he said, "My name is Nelson—B. T. Nelson. We've got a room at the Seaside Motel about a mile from here and will be staying there tonight. If you change your mind about selling the dog, give me a call, and I'll come back. I wish you would decide to sell him."

"Not a chance," replied Cap'n Tony. "Sorry."

The strangers walked to their car which was parked at the end of the dock, the boy looking back longingly at Footsie.

"Well," said Cap'n Tony, "now that's done, let's eat. I'm hungry."

He and Manuel went into the galley, Footsie following along, and soon all three of them were eating supper. When the table was cleared and the dishes washed and put back in their racks, Cap'n Tony said he would like to go visiting with Cap'n Joe on his shrimper tied up a little farther along the dock. Manuel said he and Footsie would go along, too, and they would visit with Mike.

Manuel romped for a while with the two dogs on the dock, then as it began to grow dark he left them and boarded the *Mary Lou* to sit with his grandfather and Cap'n Joe. He heard the dogs barking as they raced up and down, having a fine time stretching their legs after being on boats all day.

Suddenly Manuel realized he didn't hear them. He whistled for Footsie, but only Mike answered. Manuel stood up and happened to see the lights of a car backing away. Still whistling for Footsie, he stepped on the dock and was nearly knocked flat by Mike who came dashing at him from the darkness. But no Footsie. He walked around looking everywhere for Footsie. He called and whistled until his throat was sore, but his little black dog was nowhere to be seen.

He finally gave up the search and went back to get gramp to help him. Cap'n Tony was just leaving, and Manuel told him that Footsie had disappeared and couldn't be found. Cap'n Tony said, "Oh, he's probably found a cat around one of the warehouses here and chased him farther than he realized. He'll be back by the time we go to bed."

"I don't think so, gramp," said Manuel thoughtfully. "You know he's never left us before, and I've just remembered something. When he and Mike were running up and down the dock, I was sitting there watching them. Just as I realized I didn't hear them both barking, I saw the lights of a car backing away. You know, I'll bet anything it was those people who wanted to buy Footsie, and I'll bet they came back and stole him."

Cap'n Tony stood silently, thinking, then he said, "You just may be right, Manuel. Their name was Nelson, so they said, and they were going to be at the Seaside Motel. Let's take a run out there and talk to the night attendant."

Quickly they reached the car and started for the motel. Manuel had never seen his gramp look like this before. One minute he was praying they would find Footsie at the motel, and the next he was hoping they wouldn't. Gramp was so quiet and stern looking. Manuel knew if Mr. Nelson had stolen the puppy, gramp would get Footsie back for him, but he was afraid of what might happen.

As their car pulled into the driveway of the Seaside Motel, the attendant came around the corner of a building, carrying a pan of water. He went to a car parked there and opened the back door. As he reached inside with the water, out through the open door flashed a little furry black ball with a red collar around its neck.

"Footsie!" called Manuel, and the little dog turned so fast he almost dug up gravel in the driveway. Then he raced to Manuel and jumped up into his arms.

The attendant came over to gramp and Manuel saying, "That's your dog, isn't it?"

"Yes, he's ours," answered Gramp. "How'd you know he didn't belong in that car?"

"They didn't have 'im when they checked in this afternoon," said the attendant. "They went out for supper, then came back, and later the man went out again. When he returned, he told me he'd bought the dog, but he acted as if he wasn't telling the truth when he said it. I told him he couldn't keep the dog in the room, so he said if I'd give him some water, he'd just let the dog sleep in the car. That's what I was doing when he jumped out and started to run off. Do you want me to call the police?"

"No!" said Manuel quickly, remembering gramp's face as they drove to the motel. "I've got my dog back, and that's all I want. Come on, gramp, let's go home."

"I guess you're right, son," said gramp sighing, "but I sure would like to've punched that man right in the nose!"

Footsie leaped lightly into the front seat of the car and snuggled up close to his young master.

11.
Shrimpers Go Fishing

Cap'n Tony decided this would be his last drag for the day. His catch had been good, it was getting late, and he was tired. Jerry and Manuel lowered the net overboard then went to the pilothouse. Footsie trotted up to the bow and looked over to check on Whitey and Ditto to see if they were in their places. Satisfied that everything was under control, he joined the others and the last drag was underway.

As the *Miss Abbie* moved along slowly, Cap'n Tony thought he heard something different in the sound of the motor. He listened carefully, and sure enough, it didn't have its usual, even hum. In just a few minutes the noise became worse, and he decided he'd better pull the net in and head for home. It had been some time since he had the motor checked, and he knew something in it needed attention. Jerry and Manuel hoisted the net into the boat, and they started back.

On the way home Manuel sat thinking. "Gramp," he said, "if the *Miss Abbie* can't go out dragging tomorrow, why don't we go fishing?"

Now Cap'n Tony liked very much to fish, and he and Manuel hadn't been all summer. "When we get back to the dock and I talk to the mechanic and see what he says, we'll see," he answered.

When gramp reached the dock, he called the mechanic on the phone. As he hung up the phone, he told Manuel they would go fishing the next day. He said the mechanic could repair the boat in one day, so it would be a good time for them to take off. They made arrangements for a small boat and motor, then checked their fishing tackle.

The next morning they were up long before day, but this was their usual schedule. Gramp made some sandwiches and a thermos of coffee for their lunch. Manuel filled a jar with water for Footsie, took his little drinking pan, and the three set out for their fishing boat. Everything was loaded into the boat, then Cap'n Tony bought a quart of live shrimp to use for bait. It seemed funny to him and Manuel to be buying shrimp when usually they were selling them, and they laughed over their little joke. Gramp pulled the cord on the outboard motor a few times, then it started and off they went.

All three were as excited as if they had never been in a boat before, and Footsie barked as though it were his first trip on the water. Just after daylight when the tide was high, they reached Clam Creek on the northwest tip of Jekyll Island. Manuel threw the anchor overboard, and Footsie nearly fell out of the boat trying to catch it. The inner bait bucket was put into the water alongside the boat so the shrimp would stay alive, and Cap'n Tony cast his line, then Manuel.

Manuel got the first bite. His cork went down with a loud pop, and he snatched his rod then reeled in as fast as he could. From the way the cork went down, he thought he had a trout. When the fish was in the boat, he saw he did have a two-pound trout, and he and Cap'n Tony were glad they stopped here. Footsie sniffed at the fish, then fell over backwards when it began flopping about in the boat. He got up from the bottom of the boat and climbed on the seat. When Manuel and Cap'n Tony kept laughing at him, he looked as though he would like to say, "I didn't fall. I wasn't scared. My foot slipped," and Manuel laughed harder than ever.

Cap'n Tony pulled a fish stringer from his pocket, strung the trout on it, then put the fish overboard to keep it alive as he tied the other end to the boat.

Cap'n Tony caught the next fish, and it was a good sized trout, too. Then Manuel caught a flounder, but a crab ate his next three bait. As each fish was landed, it was added to the stringer. They fished on for several hours and both had good luck. Finally Manuel's cork

started moving away very slowly. He called to Cap'n
Tony to look at it, and Cap'n Tony said, "It might
be a bass. If it is, let him take the cork under the
water and count five. Then pull."

Manuel watched his cork until his eyes blurred. It
kept moving off and going under just a little bit.
Footsie sensed that something exciting was happening,
and he sat as close to Manuel as he could so he could
see what it was. Finally the cork went completely
under the water, and Manuel counted to five as his
grandad told him. Then he gave a mighty jerk and
started to reel in. Whatever it was on the end of the
line had other ideas, however, and it started swimming
away from the boat. The line on the reel whizzed
under Manuel's thumb until it almost burned through

the skin, but Manuel held it tight. He reeled in for a few turns then out the line went again. This kept up until Manuel felt his arms would break, but finally the fish became tired and fought less and less. Manuel wound in more and more until almost all of the line was back on the reel. He and Cap'n Tony were staring into the water to see what he had caught when suddenly they saw it. It was a big stingaree!

Gramp jumped for the dingus. This was a narrow piece of wood about a foot long with lots of nails driven close together through one end. He knew he could hit the stingaree with this and drive the nails into it; then he would be able to get the thing off the hook. Though the stingaree was tired, when he saw Cap'n Tony reaching toward him, he switched his ugly long tail with the saw-tooth barb on it and tried to hit the man with it. Gramp jumped out of the way just in time. He knew if the stingaree's tail hit him and stuck the poisoned barb into him, he would really have a bad wound.

During the excitement Footsie had been forgotten, and now he went to the side of the boat to see what was happening. Just as he did, the stingaree lashed out again with his tail. In a flash Cap'n Tony shoved Footsie out of the way. The next minute the right chance came and the dingus caught the stingaree full force. In a short while he was dead, and Gramp cut him loose from the hook, to sink to the bottom.

"Whew!" said gramp. "That was a close one, wasn't it? That fight made me hungry. S'pose we go ashore and eat in the shade?" This seemed a good idea to Manuel, for the bright summer sun was beginning to burn hotter by the hour.

After lunch they stretched out on the pine needles and live oak leaves in the quiet, cool shade. Manuel was almost asleep when Cap'n Tony whispered, "Turn your head slowly to your right and look at the doe and her fawn."

The boy did as he was told, and there, not twenty-five feet away in the clearing, stood the two deer. Two pairs of soft brown eyes met Manuel's as he stared at them, fascinated by their nearness and beauty.

In the undergrowth of palmettos and sea myrtle just beyond the deer, something moved slightly, and the startled deer leaped and disappeared. As Manuel strained to see through the brush, a wild turkey emerged warily and peered around. Seeing the two people and the dog, he clucked in alarm then timidly vanished. His colors blended so well with the sur-roundings that he was instantly camouflaged.

The spell was broken. Cap'n Tony and Manuel arose, stretching, and Cap'n Tony said, "We may as well make the most of this day, son. Long as we're here at Clam Creek and the tide is nearly low, let's dig some clams."

The man showed the boy how to look for the tiny

bit of shell which sometimes protrudes above the muddy sand. He also taught Manuel to recognize their feel under his sneakers in the shallow water of the creek. When Cap'n Tony found a clam, he dug around in the same area and usually found several more in what he called nests.

Soon they had enough for a good chowder. These were placed in the outer container of the bait bucket and all returned to the boat.

The fish bit more slowly after lunch. Manuel and Cap'n Tony sat holding their rods, listening to Footsie snoring, and both began to nod. Soon a big bumble-bee flew over the boat. It seemed to find something interesting there, and it flew up and down from bow to stern, back and forth, buzzing all the time. Footsie waked from his nap and looked to see what was making this noise. When he saw the bee, he tried to catch it, but Manuel said, "No, Footsie, no. If you catch it, you'll be sorry. No. No."

Manuel's cork started bobbing, and he forgot to watch Footsie and the bee. Right then the bee flew past Footsie just too close, and Footsie snapped and caught him! It would be hard to say which was more surprised, the bee or the pup, but Footsie knew he had the worst of it. He opened his mouth and let the bee go before you could say Jack Robinson, and the bee sailed away out of sight. Footsie shook his head a few times but was ashamed to whimper because he had disobeyed Manuel, and he didn't want his master to know the bee had stung him.

About this time the fish stopped biting entirely. Cap'n Tony said, "Looks like they've quit, son. Guess the tide must be turning. I'd just as soon go home if you're ready. How 'bout it?"

Manuel said he was agreeable, so they took in the bait bucket, pulled in the fish stringer, dragged in the anchor, and started back to the dock.

The mechanic was finishing his repair work as they reached the *Miss Abbie* and he said, "She's ready to go again in the morning, Cap'n. I'll send you my bill, and thanks for calling me."

Manuel asked gramp to let him fry some of their catch for supper, and his granddad agreed. The fish were delicious, and as Manuel gave Footsie his last bite, he asked, "Which do you like better, Footsie— fish or bumblebee?"

Footsie looked at his master brightly and pretended he didn't understand the question.

"I hope Jerry had as much fun on his day off as we did, gramp," said Manuel.

12.
Trip on a Ship

The summer was coming to an end. Manuel knew this was his last week with gramp on the *Miss Abbie*, and he still hadn't brought the boat in to the dock by himself.

Returning to port that afternoon he said suddenly, "Gramp, I wish I could live on this boat the rest of my life."

"You don't know how lucky you are, son," said Cap'n Tony. "You've had the nicest time of the year to be here. In the fall we have a lot of rain, and it's no fun then. Course we've had a few rainy days this summer, but it hasn't been bad. When the weather is hot, rain feels good. But in the fall when it gets colder, rain is just a pure mess to be in. Then winter comes, and it gets really cold, and that's something else.

"You get so cold on the water your nose, ears, and

hands feel as if they'd never get warm again. No matter how many clothes you wear, the wind seems to go right through 'em. You're nice and warm in the pilothouse, then you have to go out on deck and in two minutes you feel like you've never been warm. Your hands get so wet and numb you're not sure you're holding the shrimp. I tell you, it's no fun in the wintertime. You finally get to the point where you're really glad when the shrimp leave for warmer waters, and you can quit going out until spring."

Manuel listened to his grandad, but secretly he wondered if gramp wasn't telling him that just to keep him from feeling so badly about leaving.

When they docked, there was a man standing beside their berth. Cap'n Tony said, "There's Cap'n Louie waiting to see us. Wonder why?"

"Who's Cap'n Louie?" asked Manuel.

"He's the pilot boat captain," replied Cap'n Tony. "When the big ships come in and out of the harbor, their captains are new to these waters and don't know their way through the channel. Cap'n Louie owns the pilot boat. You've seen it. He steers the ships in and out. If the ship is coming in, he and his striker go out together on the pilot boat to meet it. Cap'n Louie gets aboard the ship and brings it in, and his striker takes the pilot boat in. When the ship is outgoing, Cap'n Louie steers it, and the striker takes the pilot boat. When the ship is clear of the channel and out in open water, Cap'n Louie transfers from the ship to the pilot boat and comes back to his dock. Wonder what he wants?" But he didn't have to wait long to find out. As soon as the *Miss Abbie* was tied up, Cap'n Louie came aboard.

"Heard your grandson has been on your boat this summer," said Cap'n Louie. "There's a foreign ship in port that I'm taking out early tomorrow morning, and I wondered if he'd like to come along with us. It's not often the captain of a big ship will allow me to take anyone along, but this one says I can take the boy if he'd like to go."

"How 'bout it, Manuel?" asked Cap'n Tony. "Would you like to go with Louie?"

"Yes, sir!" cried Manuel. "I surely would!"

Footsie barked his acceptance of the invitation, but Cap'n Louie said, "No, dog, you can't go. To get from the ship to the pilot boat we have to go down a rope ladder, and you couldn't do that. You stay on board the *Miss Abbie* with Tony, and I'll bring your master back to you tomorrow afternoon. What time do you usually leave the dock, Tony?"

"Around two thirty or quarter of three," replied Cap'n Tony.

"I'm scheduled to leave at three," said Cap'n Louie, "so that works out fine. You bring the boy over to my dock just before you're ready to take off, and I'll look after him. If we get back before you do in the afternoon, he can stay with me until you come for him."

"I'll have him there," said Cap'n Tony. "Sure do

appreciate your taking him, Louie, for it'll be a trip he won't forget."

"Thought he'd like to go," said Cap'n Louie. "That's why I asked the ship's captain about it. Well, I'll see you in the morning, Manuel," he said as he left.

Manuel was so excited he could hardly eat his supper. The trip on the big ship was all he could talk about, and Cap'n Tony listened smilingly.

About 2:30 the next morning gramp drove Manuel to the pilot boat dock and left him with Cap'n Louie. All around them was the hustle and bustle of a ship's sailing. Crewmen were calling back and forth from the ship to the dock, and all this added to the din. Cap'n Louie took Manuel across the gangplank and up to the bridge of the ship where he introduced the boy to the captain. Manuel was so impressed that he sat quietly while Cap'n Louie gave orders. Soon the huge ship's load of resin barrels was completed, it was backed away from the dock, and they were underway.

Then the questions started. Where had the ship come from? Where was it bound? What cargo did it have aboard? By the time Cap'n Louie piloted it through the channel down the river and out into the open sea, Manuel had been all over the ship from stem to stern and back again. It was the biggest thing afloat he'd ever been on, and the *Miss Abbie* looked like a bathtub toy when they passed her.

As the pilot boat came up close to the ship to take

off Cap'n Louie and Manuel, it seemed very small and an awfully long way down. A rope ladder was put over the side, and as the big ship rolled in the waves, the ladder swung out and in from the side.

Cap'n Louie asked anxiously, "Do you think you can make it, boy?"

"Sure," Manuel replied confidently, but secretly he was scared. He wondered if he could land on the deck of the little pilot boat when they reached the bottom of the rope ladder, or if he would fall between it and the ship. Cap'n Louie said, "I'll go first, you come one step later. That way, I'll be beneath you and can catch you if you slip. When we get to the bottom of the ladder, hold on till I say jump. Then don't look around—don't wait a second—just jump."

They climbed over the side of the ship and slowly made their way down the tossing, swinging, bumping ladder. Cap'n Louie called, "Jump!" and Manuel did. He landed on the deck of the pilot boat, and Cap'n Louie steadied him.

All the way back to the dock Manuel was talking about his trip and what might've happened. Cap'n Louie smiled and said, "I tell you the truth, boy. After I invited you to go along on this trip, I got to thinking about what could happen, and though I hate to admit it now, I was sorry I asked you. But you behaved exactly right on the ship, and you jumped from the ladder when I told you. If you hadn't done what I told you, you could've fallen between the ship and the pilot boat, and that's what had me scared."

"Were you scared, Cap'n Louie?" laughed Manuel. "You surely didn't show it if you were. But I was so scared I was certain you could hear my teeth chattering and my heart thumping as we came down the ladder."

"Was that your heart I heard, boy?" roared Cap'n Louie. "By golly, I thought it was the ladder bumping the side of the ship!"

Cap'n Tony was waiting when they reached the dock, and he listened over and over to the exciting story. He thanked Cap'n Louie again for taking the boy, and they left to return to the *Miss Abbie*. Footsie was waiting for his master on the deck and greeted him as though he had been gone a month instead of a few hours.

All that evening Manuel thought about Cap'n Louie steering the big ship, his striker taking out the pilot boat, and Cap'n Tony and Jerry piloting the *Miss Abbie*. As Cap'n Tony turned out the light, Manuel sighed deeply and prayed a tiny prayer, "Lord, please let me bring *Miss Abbie* in just once by myself. Time is getting short."

13.
The Last Day

At the beginning of summer, three months on the *Miss Abbie* seemed like a wonderfully long time. But now, the last day, it seemed more like three weeks, instead.

Manuel's heart was heavy all day with the thought that this was his last trip to sea. His muscles were hard, and his skin was brown. According to the way his clothes fit, he must have grown an inch or two during the summer. But he wasn't thinking of any of this as the day wore on.

After lunch, one of the other shrimp boats pulled up alongside the *Miss Abbie,* and the captain said, "Tony, my radio has quit working. I don't know a thing about repairing it and neither does my striker. Does Jerry know how to work with radios, and if so, could you spare him to have a look at it?"

"I know something about them," said Jerry, "but I don't know whether I can fix yours or not. I'll be glad to see what I can do if Cap'n Tony is willing to let me try."

"Sure, Jerry, go see what you can find out," said Cap'n Tony. Then he glanced at his watch. "It's so near the end of our trawling day, why don't you stay aboard and go in with them? We're going to make just one more drag, and Manuel and I can work together on the sorting and heading. That will give you longer to tinker, and we really don't need you."

Jerry swung aboard the boat and away it went, leaving Manuel and gramp to take care of the last haul.

"Drag a little longer than usual, gramp," begged Manuel. "This is my last one, you know, and I want it to be the biggest of the whole summer."

So gramp did as Manuel asked and up, down, and around the sound went the *Miss Abbie*. Finally they decided the time had come to pull in the net, so Manuel took care of that. It was a huge catch. Cap'n Tony put the boat in neutral, and they drifted slowly while he and Manuel worked heading the shrimp.

Suddenly Cap'n Tony cried out in pain, "Oh! That dratted catfish!" and Manuel looked up to see both his grandad's hands bleeding badly.

"What happened, gramp?" asked Manuel as he looked with fright at his grandad.

"It's been so long since I've done this separating I guess I got careless," said gramp as he winced in pain.

102

"There was a catfish mixed with the shrimp, and I didn't see him in time. He stuck his fins in both my hands."

"Now I see why you warned me about them," said Manuel. "Don't worry, gramp. Go lie down in the cabin, and I'll get us back to port."

"I'm afraid I'm going to have to, Manuel," said gramp. "I've got bad cuts on both my hands, and I'm beginning to get sick at my stomach, too. I'll wrap a towel around the cuts to keep from bleeding on everything. You hail the next boat that comes by, and they'll help us."

Manuel scanned the ocean as gramp disappeared into the cabin. There was not a shrimp boat in sight! Their last drag was unusually long, and all the others had left for home. He and gramp were alone out there on the big Atlantic, and gramp was hurt. He needed a doctor, and there wasn't time to call in for help.

Quickly he decided what to do. He would take the *Miss Abbie* in himself!

His one thought now was to get gramp to a doctor. Carefully he placed the box in front of the wheel, climbed up on it, and slowly put the boat in gear. He was so frightened the blood pounded in his ears, and his knees were so shaky he could hardly stand. He tried to remember everything gramp had told him about steering, and as the *Miss Abbie* slowly started back to dock, Manuel gradually calmed down.

Footsie seemed to know that Manuel was in trouble,

103

and he stood as close as he could to the box on which Manuel was standing.

Manuel lined up the buoys as gramp had told him, and gradually the boat began to go more evenly. The wake behind her became smooth and even, and Manuel thought, "If gramp could see this, he'd be proud of me."

He began to get confidence in himself, so he pushed the throttle ahead a little more. The *Miss Abbie* seemed to know that she was in new hands. Never had the motor run more smoothly or the wheel responded so easily. Almost before he could believe it, Manuel saw the dock ahead and knew that his final, real test was before him. Running the boat in open water was one thing, but docking it was another!

Carefully he slowed the motor, and doing exactly as he had seen gramp do so many times, he gently eased the *Miss Abbie* in to the dock as though he had done it all his life! He jumped onto the dock, tied up the line, then sped to Cap'n Joe.

In less time than it takes to tell, the doctor was there. Cap'n Tony's hands were treated and bandaged, and as the last knot of the bandage was tied, gramp said, "How did we get back here, Manuel?"

"Why, gramp, you know I brought us in," replied Manuel. "When your hands were hurt, you went to the cabin and lay down. I had to bring us in 'cause Jerry was gone and you were hurt, and Footsie certainly couldn't do it! So I brought us back, that's all."

"I must've passed out," said gramp. "The last thing I remember was going to the cabin. My goodness! You brought the *Miss Abbie* in all by yourself on your first try? If I'd known you were that good, I'd have had you doing it long before now! You sure you didn't knock the dock down or cave in her bow?" But he laughed as he said it!

"I didn't even take a scratch of paint off," Manuel said proudly, and he grinned. "Footsie, the *Miss Abbie,* and I did the job just right."

"And now you'll be leaving just as you're getting to be of some use to me in steering," complained gramp. "You going to take the dog or leave him with me?"

A lump came into Manuel's throat, and he stood silent. He looked first at Footsie then at gramp. "He loves the sea as much as I do," he said finally, "so I guess I'd better leave him with you. I can come down here and see him some time, so it won't be like I'm giving him up entirely."

"Why don't we let Footsie decide for himself?" asked gramp wisely. "He loves the sea, yes, but he also loves you. Footsie," said gramp, taking the dog's head in his hands, "summer is over, and Manuel has to leave the sea to go back to school. You can stay with me, or you can go with him. We're going to let you decide which you want to do."

The dog looked deep into Cap'n Tony's eyes, then the bandaged hands came away slowly from the little black face. For a moment the dog continued to sit in front of Cap'n Tony, then he stood up and walked over to Manuel. He sat down on the cabin deck and looked up. If he had said, "I'm going with you. You are my choice," he couldn't have made it more plain.

"You made a wise selection, Footsie," said gramp. "I want to tell you, Manuel, that you have a job waiting for you on this boat every summer for as long as you want it. And you too, Footsie," he added as the boy and the dog leaped lightly over the rail to the dock.

For further reading—

PAUL: GOD'S ADVENTURER. By Robbie Trent. The author has sensitively reconstructed Paul's early years, interpreting what the Bible says about Paul's background and what other authentic sources reveal about the life of a typical Jewish boy during those times. Then the easy-to-read narrative evolves into the actual Bible story. Illustrated. #80381 (hardback)

SHELLS FROM THE SEA. By Robbie Trent. Lovely pencil drawings enhance this charming account of a visit to the seashore. A mother and child find more than a dozen different shells—periwinkle, starfish, sand dollar, seahorse, conch. The child learns about the wonders of God's creation and His concern for all things great and small. #80421 (hardback)

SUKI AND THE INVISIBLE PEACOCK. By Joyce Blackburn. Suki, a most delightful and imaginative Japanese-American girl, wants a best friend all her own. What happens when that Best Friend turns out to be an invisible peacock will enchant and delight any child. Illustrated. Suitable for children ages 4–8. #98058 (quality paperback)

SUKI AND THE OLD UMBRELLA. By Joyce Blackburn. Suki gets into trouble with her conscience when she "borrows" an umbrella from the school janitor. Luckily, her wise Best Friend, the invisible peacock, can help her out of such a predicament. Illustrated. Suitable for children ages 4–8. #98057 (quality paperback)

SUKI AND THE MAGIC SAND DOLLAR. By Joyce Blackburn. The delightful, warm story of little Suki Gosho. This is a "learning" book in which the author teaches a fundamental respect for scientific discovery, plus a reverence for the Creator. Suki comes to love persons of another race without ever thinking of them as "different." Illustrated. Suitable for children ages 4–8. #98059 (quality paperback)

SUKI AND THE WONDER STAR. By Joyce Blackburn. She's grown a little; she's in the fourth grade. Her friend Butch is back, too. And there's a new boy—a bright, competitive Spanish-speaking boy named Manuel. Suki is feeling left out because Butch and Manuel have become close friends. In a special dream about the Wonder Star, she learns to accept Manuel and appreciate the talents of others who aren't just like herself. Suitable for ages 5–10. #98056 (quality paperback)